SAMANTHA'S WINTER PARTY

SAMANTHA · 1904

BY VALERIE TRIPP

ILLUSTRATIONS DAN ANDREASEN

VIGNETTES SUSAN MCALILEY

THE AMERICAN GIRLS COLLECTION®

Published by Pleasant Company Publications
Previously published in *American Girl*® magazine
© Copyright 1999 by Pleasant Company
For information, address: Book Editor, Pleasant Company Publications,
8400 Fairway Place, P.O. Box 620998, Middleton, WI 53562.

Printed in Hong Kong.
99 00 01 02 03 04 05 06 C&C 10 9 8 7 6 5

The American Girls Collection®
is a trademark of Pleasant Company.

Edited by Nancy Holyoke and Michelle Jones
Designed by Laura Moberly
Art Directed by Kirstin Beckman and Laura Moberly

Library of Congress Cataloging-in-Publication Data

Tripp, Valerie, 1951-
Samantha's winter party / by Valerie Tripp ;
illustrations, Dan Andreasen ; vignettes, Susan McAliley. — 1st ed.
p. cm. — (The American girls collection)
Summary: When her friend Nellie, the servant girl from next door, does
not show up for ice skating as usual, Samantha is afraid that Nellie will
not come to her party because she cannot afford to bring presents.
Includes a section on ice skating in the early 1900s.

ISBN 1-56247-766-8.
[1. Friendship—Fiction. 2. Ice Skating—Fiction.
3. Orphans—Fiction.]
I. Andreasen, Dan, ill. II. Title. III. Series.
PZ7.T7363Gi   1999   [Fic]—dc21   98-34557   CIP   AC

The
AMERICAN GIRLS
COLLECTION
™

OTHER AMERICAN GIRLS
SHORT STORIES:

PICTURE CREDITS
The following individuals and organizations have generously given
permission to reprint illustrations contained in "Looking Back":
p. 32—Illustration by C. H. Kuechler, 1895, Mary Evans Picture Library;
p. 33—Museum of the City of New York; p. 34—The World Figure Skating Museum;
p. 35—Currier & Ives, Charles Parsons, Winter: The Skating Pond, 1862. Museum of
the City of New York, J. Clarence Davies Collection, 29.100.1868 (bottom);
p. 36—Corbis Bettmann; p. 37, 38, 39, 40—The World Figure Skating Museum;
p. 41—Twentieth Century Fox, Courtesy Kobal; p. 42—Photography by Jamie Young.

TABLE OF CONTENTS

SAMANTHA'S FAMILY

GRANDMARY
*Samantha's grandmother,
who wants her to be
a young lady.*

UNCLE GARD
*Samantha's favorite uncle,
who calls her Sam.*

SAMANTHA
*A nine-year-old orphan
who lives with her wealthy
grandmother.*

CORNELIA
*An old-fashioned beauty who
has newfangled ideas.*

NELLIE
*The girl who lives—
and works—next door.*

SAMANTHA'S
WINTER PARTY

L et's race!" Samantha called. Across
   Culpepper's Pond she skated, going
so fast she felt as if she were flying. Ida,
Helen, Ruth, and Nellie were right
behind her, their skates flashing. The race
ended in a tie as all five girls skidded up
to the edge of the pond at the same time.
They collapsed on the bench together in a
breathless, giggling heap.

"Jeepers!" said Ida after they'd
untangled themselves. "My fingers are so

stiff I can hardly undo my skates!"

"I hope it stays this cold," said Samantha. "Won't it be fun to skate during our Christmas vacation?"

"Oh, yes!" The other girls agreed happily.

It had been the coldest winter any-one could remember. For weeks now,

Culpepper's Pond had been frozen solid. Skating was all the rage. Almost every day, Samantha, Ida, Helen, and Ruth burst out of Miss Crampton's Academy with their schoolbooks under their arms and their ice skates slung over their shoulders and rushed straight to the pond.

This Friday afternoon skating was especially fun because Samantha's friend Nellie was able to come, too. Nellie was a good skater. She was teaching the others how to skate backward and do figure eights. All the girls liked it when Nellie came to the pond, but she could only come on Mondays and Fridays. Nellie and her parents were servants for Mrs. Van Sicklen, and Nellie usually had to work.

Samantha looked out at the crowd as she unbuckled her skates. In their bright hats and coats, the skaters looked like a flock of colorful birds, swooping, skimming, and swirling across the ice. Two of the skaters left the crowd and skated toward the bench. Samantha saw that they were Edith and Clarisse, who also went to Miss Crampton's Academy. "Hello," Samantha said politely as the girls stopped.

But Edith didn't waste time with politeness. "I'm having a party Monday after school, and my mother is making me invite all the girls in my class at Miss Crampton's," she said. "So that means all of you—except

Nellie, of course—have to come. We're going to practice our song for the Christmas pageant."

"Monday?" asked Samantha.

Helen blurted out what Samantha was thinking: "But that means we'll miss skating with Nellie!"

Edith sniffed. "Well, then, you needn't stay at the party very long. That way you'll have time to skate with your friend the servant girl."

Clarisse had been staring at Nellie's skates. They were very old, and the blades and buckles were rusty. Now Clarisse whispered something to Edith, and they both smirked. As they skated away,

Clarisse said in a loud voice, "I think it's pathetic the way that Nellie is always trying to keep up with her betters!"

Nellie quickly bent down to gather up her schoolbooks, but Samantha could see that her cheeks were red. Samantha was so angry at Edith and Clarisse for hurting Nellie's feelings she wished she could punch them! "Don't pay any attention to those nincompoops, Nellie," she said.

"That's right," said Helen. She crossed her eyes and stuck her tongue out at the girls' backs.

"I wish I didn't have to go to Edith's party," said Ida. "It won't be fun."

"I know!" said Samantha, with enthusiasm. "Let's have our own special party next Friday!"

"Oh, yes, let's!" agreed Helen and
Ida and Ruth.

"We'll skate first, and then we can
have the party at my house," said
Samantha. "I'm sure Grandmary
will allow it. We can sing carols
and eat cookies and drink cocoa—"

"And we can give each other
presents!" Helen piped up. "Special
presents for our most special friends."

"Yes!" agreed all the girls—all except
Nellie.

Nellie was very quiet. Immediately,
Samantha realized why. *Nellie has no
money. She cannot possibly buy presents for
us*, she thought. *Oh dear! I brought up the*

*party to make Nellie feel better, and now I'm
afraid it's made her feel worse!*

Samantha thought hard as Ida, Helen,
and Ruth chattered on about the party
and joked about the presents they were
going to give each other. After the other
girls said goodbye and headed home,
Samantha smiled at her friend.

"Nellie, I have a good idea!" she said.
"Why don't you and I get together and
make presents for the other girls? Wouldn't
that be fun?"

Nellie looked uncertain. "Do you
think homemade presents will be all
right?" she asked. "All the other girls
will have store-bought."

"Good gifts don't have to cost

money!" said Samantha. "Once I saw someone make really nice Christmas corsages out of pinecones."

"Corsages!" said Nellie. "That's so grown-up! Do you remember how to make them?"

"I think so," said Samantha. "Anyway, how hard can it be? Let's meet tomorrow afternoon and collect a lot of pinecones."

Nellie smiled. "I'll bring a basket," she said.

A light snow was falling the next afternoon as Samantha and Nellie walked through the woods just behind the Van Sicklens' house, filling Nellie's

9

basket with pinecones.

"Be careful where you step," Nellie warned Samantha. "It's marshy. There are puddles as big as small ponds in here."

Samantha scraped a bit of the snow away with the toe of her boot. "The puddles are all frozen," she said. "See? There's ice under the snow." She looked around. "It's pretty here, isn't it?"

"Pretty and *cold*," said Nellie, shivering. "Let's go inside."

The girls hurried to Samantha's house. It was cozy in the kitchen. On the table, Samantha had carefully set out everything they needed to make their corsages. They began eagerly, talking as they worked.

"The other girls are going to be so pleased that we made our presents for them all by ourselves," said Samantha.

"It will be a surprise!" said Nellie happily.

But making the corsages was a lot harder than Samantha had remembered. The gold paint was globby. The cheery sprigs of holly pricked their fingers. The Christmas-red ribbon wouldn't stay tied in bows. The lacy paper snowflakes refused to stick on the pinecones. Samantha and Nellie grew quieter and quieter as they became more and more discouraged.

After hours of struggle, the kitchen table was sticky with glue and globs of gold paint. It was littered with short bits of ribbon, crushed holly sprigs, and clumps of wadded-up paper. Samantha wrinkled her brow and held up a mangled-looking, splotchy, gluey pinecone. "I must have forgotten some important step," she said. "This doesn't look anything like a corsage."

"Mine doesn't, either," Nellie said. She sighed. "The corsages were a nice idea, Samantha," she went on kindly. "But let's be honest. They're not working."

"What if we put jingle bells on them?" asked Samantha. "I've got some we could use."

But Nellie shook her head and grinned a little. "We'd need something more than jingle bells to make these look

12

any good," she said. "We'd need something *magic*."

"You're right," Samantha admitted. "We might as well throw this stuff away."

In silence, the girls swept the crumpled paper, wrinkled ribbons, and globby gold pinecones off the table and into Nellie's basket. "Maybe we could try

making something else for the girls,"
Samantha suggested at last. "Or maybe
we could *find* something—"

"No," Nellie said firmly. "I know
you're trying to help me, Samantha, but
you can't." She tossed a pinecone into
the basket and dusted off her hands.
"Clarisse was right," she said. "Servant
girls shouldn't try to 'keep up.' I don't
have any money to spend the way you
and your friends do."

Samantha felt helpless. "But you'll
come to the party on Friday, won't you,
Nellie?" she asked. "The party will be the
most fun. Presents don't matter. No one
expects . . . I mean, no one will care if
you don't give—"

Nellie interrupted. "*I* would care," she said simply. She picked up the basket of scraps. "I'll get rid of this," she said. And then she left.

Samantha slumped at the table. She had hurt Nellie's pride. Now Nellie might not come to the party. It seemed the more Samantha tried to make things better, the more she made things worse.

❧

Samantha, Helen, Ruth, and Ida had rushed to the pond after Edith's party on Monday, but they could not find Nellie. No one had seen her skating that afternoon.

"Gosh!" said Ruth. "Why isn't Nellie here? She knew we were coming. She's never missed a Monday afternoon before!"

"I sure hope she comes Friday," said Helen. "The party won't be fun without her."

Samantha said nothing. She knew why Nellie wasn't there. *She's avoiding us*, Samantha thought. *Oh, I've got to talk to her!*

After skating, Samantha went straight to the Van Sicklens' house and knocked on the front door. Nellie's father opened it. "Why, hello, Samantha," he said. "How may I help you today?"

"Please, Mr. O'Malley," said Samantha. "May I see Nellie?"

Mr. O'Malley seemed to hesitate, but

then he smiled. "Come in and wait in the hall," he said.

"Thank you," said Samantha. As she stood waiting, she could hear Mr. O'Malley talking to Nellie in the kitchen.

"Samantha's here," he said.

"Oh, no!" Samantha heard Nellie say.

Samantha's heart sank. Nellie didn't want to see her!

When Nellie appeared, she seemed nervous. "Hello, Samantha," she said.

"Nellie, we missed you at the pond," said Samantha.

"Oh!" said Nellie. " I . . . I was busy."

Samantha had never seen Nellie so stiff and unfriendly! "Oh, Nellie," she

Samantha had never seen Nellie so stiff and unfriendly!

burst out. "Can't we go in the kitchen and talk for a while?"

"No!" said Nellie quickly. "We can't. I . . . uh, I better get back to work." She opened the front door. "Thank you for coming, Samantha. You'd better go now."

Before Samantha knew it, she was back outside. Even more bitter than the cold was the feeling that she had lost her friend. There could be no doubt about it— Nellie did not want to see Samantha or talk to her. Samantha trudged home sadly.

The day of the party was dreary and cold. After school, when the girls got to Culpepper's Pond, Samantha was sorry but not surprised to see that Nellie was not there. The girls skated without her, but after a while Helen said, "Maybe Nellie's waiting for us at your house, Samantha. Shall we go see?"

They walked up the hill, dropped their skates in a pile on the front porch, and filed inside.

Nellie wasn't there.

"Well," said Samantha glumly. "We might as well have some refreshments."

As the girls were getting their first cups of cocoa, Nellie appeared at the door to the parlor. She had a big red bow in her hair and a big smile on her face.

"Nellie!" the girls cried in delight as they rushed to her. "You're here!"

"Oh, we were so afraid you weren't coming!" said Ida.

"Now that you've come, the party can begin!" said Helen.

Samantha was too relieved and delighted to say anything. She sat at the piano and played "The Twelve Days of Christmas" as loudly as she could. The girls got the words all mixed up. No one could remember if it was the lords who were leaping or the ladies, but no one seemed to mind. And Ruth sang "five goooolden rings" in such a funny, warbling voice that they all collapsed with laughter. Singing made them hungry, so they ate cookies and drank more steaming cups of cocoa beside the fire.

"Now!" said Ida, setting down her empty cup. "Let's open our presents."

Samantha watched Nellie carefully out of the corner of her eye. Nellie hadn't brought any packages, but she watched her friends exchange gifts with happy, glowing eyes.

"Here, Nellie," said Samantha, handing her a big box. "We all chipped in to buy this gift for you."

"Thank you," said Nellie politely. She opened the box, and her face grew pink. "Oh, *thank you!*" she said again as she lifted out a beautiful pair of ice skates. "What a wonderful surprise!"

Then suddenly Nellie

22

"Here, Nellie," said Samantha, handing her a big box.
"We all chipped in to buy this gift for you."

23

stood up, and holding her skates to her chest, she said, "Now you must all get your skates and come with me, because I have a surprise for *you.*"

Giggling and chattering, the girls put on their coats. They followed Nellie out the door and picked up their skates on the porch. The sun was just setting. The sky was dark purple streaked with pink, and a few early stars were out. Nellie led the curious and excited girls through the twilight to the woods behind the Van Sicklens' house. When at last she stopped among the trees, her friends all gasped in amazement at what they saw.

"Oooooooh!" they sighed.

The woods were transformed! Nellie

had swept the snow off the ice so that all the small, perfect ponds were clear. One pond led to another, like shiny stepping stones made of mirrors. The ponds were rimmed by candles planted in the snow and by small bouquets of holly sprigs. Nellie had hung lanterns from the largest tree branches, and their light glowed against the wintry dusk. Glittering gold pinecones and lacy paper snowflakes hung from the trees, too, and bits of red ribbon that fluttered and danced.

"It's like an enchanted forest," whispered Samantha, and all the girls murmured in agreement.

At that moment, Mr. O'Malley

*"It's like an enchanted forest," whispered Samantha,
and all the girls murmured in agreement.*

appeared, carrying his violin. As the girls strapped on their skates, he began to play a waltz, and the thin notes floated clear and fine on the night air.

Samantha skated next to Nellie. "It's so beautiful, Nellie!" she said.

Nellie beamed. "My dad helped me," she said. "We came out here together early this morning, before sunrise. He checked the ice to be sure it was safe, and he helped me put up the decorations, too. But it was my idea! I made the decorations out of the scraps from our corsage project. I was making them the day you came to see me, Samantha, and that's why I couldn't let you come into the kitchen. I wanted my gift for you to be a surprise!

"It's the most wonderful surprise
I've ever seen!" said Samantha. "I don't
know how you ever did it."

Nellie smiled and twirled in a little
circle on the ice. "Oh," she said. "It was
just a little magic."

VALERIE TRIPP

At 9   Now

One very cold winter afternoon, my daughter led me to a spot in the woods where she'd found a series of small ponds—frozen puddles, really—among the trees. We didn't have ice skates, so we slipped and slid from pond to pond in our boots. It was so pretty there in the woods, and the ponds seemed made just for us. That's where I got the idea for this story.

Valerie Tripp has written twenty-one books in The American Girls Collection, including three about Samantha.

Looking
Back
1904

A PEEK INTO
THE PAST

Skating costumes made it hard to jump and spin.

When Samantha was growing up, ice-skating was all the rage. People loved to strap on their skates and show off their fancy footwork. And it was some-thing almost every-one could do—all they needed was a pair of skates and a frozen lake or pond. People who weren't

A skate chair in Central Park

good skaters could sit in skate chairs and be pushed across the ice.

People have skated for thousands of years. The earliest known skate, made of animal bone, is said to be over two thousand years old! Skating became much easier as skates were made of wood, iron, and finally steel in the early 1800s. These early skates had straps that buckled around a skater's shoes or boots. The skaters moved stiffly because they didn't want their shoes or boots to slip out of the skates. They concentrated on carving complicated patterns such as the "rattlesnake" or a "rosette" with their sharp blades. One skater even etched an entire love letter to his sweetheart in the ice!

In 1850 a strapless skate was invented. It had blades that clipped right into the boot. Now skaters could twist, turn, spin, and leap without losing their blades. Over the next few years, lots of changes were made in skate design. The front of the blade changed from a curve to a sharp point. This let skaters perform fancier moves. Skates with *toe picks*, or sharp teeth in the front

Rattlesnake

This ladies' skate was $2.38 in 1902.

of the blade, also appeared. Toe picks helped skaters with jumps and spins. Around the turn of the century, skates like those we have today, with the blade and the boot attached as one piece, were invented.

In New York City, many people skated on the lake in Central Park. When the park was built, it attracted almost forty thousand skaters every day. New

Ice-skating in Central Park became popular in the 1850s.

Yorkers knew the lakes were safe to skate on when a red ball was up in the bell tower next to the lake.

In the 1890s, an indoor ice rink called Empire City was built in New York. It was the size of a football field. The rink had music playing and was lit with gas lights so skaters could skate at night.

When skaters skated at night in the

Empire City

country, they carried a skater's lamp. The lamp had a chain with a ring that hooked onto a skater's finger. The light helped skaters avoid obstacles on the ice like sticks, rough spots, and other people!

A skater's lamp

Around 1900, women began to compete in ice-skating. One of the first was Madge Syers of Great Britain. She entered the all-male world championship in 1902. Madge defeated two men to place second in the competition! The next year, skating officials stopped women from competing against men because their long dresses

prevented judges from seeing their feet. In 1905 a separate ladies' championship was established, and Madge won in 1906 and 1907. A year later, she became the first female Olympic figure-skating gold medalist.

Madge Syers was the first great female skater.

At the 1920 Olympic Games, a judge warned American skater Theresa Weld that it was not proper for a woman to perform jumps because her skirt would fly up to her knees. If she did jump, she would lose points. Theresa didn't pay any attention to the judge and put a small jump in her program. She won her free-skating program and a bronze medal overall.

Then in 1924 figure skating was changed again, this time by an 11-year-old girl. At the Olympic Games, Sonja Henie wore a knee-length skirt, the style for a girl her age. The shorter skirt allowed her to spin and

Sonja was 6 years old when she got her first pair of skates.

jump like male skaters. At the time, jumps were not considered ladylike. The shocked judges gave Sonja last place! Four years later, Sonja surprised the judges again by combining dance patterns and ice-skating. But this time the judges liked her new approach, and she took home the first of her ten world titles. Sonja began to be called the "Pavlova of the Ice" after her idol, ballerina Anna Pavlova. Sonja's programs encouraged all women skaters to

Sonja Henie at the St. Moritz Olympics in 1928

40

skate more athletic programs. Women began jumping and spinning as they never had before! By 1930, Sonja was everywhere—even in Hollywood movies. Her influence is still seen today. Since

Sonja didn't like black skates, she wore beige ones instead. When her competitors copied her, Sonja wore white skates. Most girls since then have worn white skates, too!

MAKE SNOW CANDLES

Light up your own enchanted forest!

Nellie wanted to surprise Samantha and her friends by creating a winter wonderland around Culpepper's Pond. She hung lanterns, gold pinecones with bits of red ribbon, and lacy paper snowflakes in the trees. In the snow around the pond, she set candles in small bouquets of holly sprigs. Make your own enchanted forest with these snow candles.

YOU WILL NEED:

 An adult to help you

Snow

Spoon

Paraffin wax (1-pound box)

Old crayons

Empty tin can

Large saucepan

Water

Potholders

Candle wicking, 4 inches long

Hint: If you don't have snow where you live, try making sand candles. Fill a plastic container with sand. You can buy sand at discount marts and lumberyards. Then follow the steps using damp sand instead of snow.

1. Prepare your snow mold. Find a spot where the snow is at least a foot deep, and cold and dry enough to keep its shape.

2. Make a hole that is about 3 inches wide and 3 inches deep in the snow. This is your mold. Experiment with different shapes if you like. When your mold is ready, it's time to melt your wax.

3. Put the wax and crayons into the can. Then put the can in the saucepan. Fill the saucepan with water until it comes halfway up the side of the can.

4. Have an adult boil the water in the saucepan. Watch the wax carefully. Once it has melted, have an adult pour the wax into your snow mold.

5. Insert the wick in the center of the wax. Hold onto the wick for a few minutes until the wax cools and hardens enough to hold the wick straight. Let the candle cool for about an hour.

6. Carefully dig the candle out of the hole. Trim the wick. Scrape off any bumps on the bottom so your candle will stand up, and it's ready to light.

BUSINESS REPLY MAIL
FIRST-CLASS MAIL   PERMIT NO. 1137   MIDDLETON WI

POSTAGE WILL BE PAID BY ADDRESSEE

PO BOX 620497
MIDDLETON WI 53562-9940